The

Star Pirate

A.C. Winfield

The Star Pirate
Text © 2013 A.C. Winfield
Cover & illustrations © A.C. Winfield

ISBN-13: 978-1494202507
ISBN-10: 1494202506

For Star x

Acknowledgements

Firstly, I would like to thank my mum who has stood by me in everything I do, particularly on days when I am rambling on about Star Bears and pirates – asking if we can go and see steam ships and explore manors – and for putting up with my random ideas.

Also a huge, huge thank you goes out to my big sis and her family across the waves. Star, this one is for you. Thank you for believing in me and my characters. Without you, I don't think they would have come alive nor expressed themselves as loudly as they do now.

To Joy Shallcross for helping a huge amount by reading through *The Star Pirate* and understanding what I meant when my words, unlike in Ebony's little book, misbehaved themselves. For boosting my confidence, so I could start telling the world about a little girl called Ebony.

To Vickie Johnstone, my fantastic editor, who did her job brilliantly without losing my voice. Thank you!

A big thank you goes out to the rest of my family and friends for treading this rocky, long, winding path with me, and for getting out the pompoms when I needed them the most.

Last, but by no means least, thanks to you, the reader, for choosing to take your time to read this book. Without you, Ebony's world would not shine so bright.

Thank you, A x

The Star Pirate

*E*bony was not like any other child in the mysterious land of Ia. The girl was brought into this world during a time of need and even though neither she nor the people knew it, she would be Ia's only hope in the time of the Great War. An innocent soul caught up between the clashes of the Humans and the Eternals, Ebony shone the brightest among them all, for she was the daughter of the land, the sea and the stars.

The girl knew she shouldn't go into her grandfather's study, but every once in a while she would find herself drawn to that place. It was really a bedroom and Ebony could have questioned why, out of all the rooms in the manor, her grandfather had chosen that particular one to use as his study, but it led into the most magnificent place in the whole of Ia – the library.

It was not the fact that she could sit in one of the comfy window seats with a view across the bay to read her favourite story, chosen from the numerous books stacked shelf after shelf, that the library was Ebony's preferred room. No, out of the many rooms in Ladon Manor where the girl lived with her grandfather, the library was her favourite because of its painted ceiling.

It was illustrated with a starry night sky, where two Star Bears, Ursa Major and Ursa Minor, danced with their friend, the mighty Star Dragon, Ladon.

The girl dreamt of this room often and one book in particular seemed to speak to her. "Ebony, open me. Open me, Ebony," it whispered over and over again while she slept.

That morning, once again, the girl found that she couldn't resist temptation. She poked her head around the corner of the door to check the coast was clear, sneaked inside the study, and slowly and quietly closed the door behind her. Ebony moved the narrow ladder on its tiny wheels, which squeaked loudly as she dragged it across to the correct place. The sound made her glance behind, for she didn't want to be discovered.

On days like this, Ebony would sit on the window seat for hours on end, reading the same tattered, ancient book with most of its crinkled pages falling out. The small volume fitted perfectly in her little hands. It rested most of the time, when she was not reading it, on the topmost, dustiest shelf in her grandfather's library all on its own.

3

always felt sorry for the book. "Why are ᴏur own?" she would ask it.

time the girl finished reading, she placed the n the bottom shelf of the bookcase with the others to keep it company. But the next time she sneaked into the library, she would find it on the top shelf again, all alone. Taking the tattered, old thing down once more, Ebony would find it dusty, as if it had been up there for all time. The girl would smooth the surface of the cover delicately with her tiny fingers until every lump, bump, notch and dent was dust free.

Ebony loved this book so much because the pictures and the stories told inside were amazing. Normally, she found reading difficult as the words would jump around, but this story was different; her favourite book, with most of its pages falling out, was kind to her. The girl came to think of the volume as her friend as its strange little words didn't jump around like the others did, which she thought was kind of them.

Sometimes Ebony would hear someone approaching while she was in the library, but, luckily, she had found a good hiding place. When the girl heard someone walking in the echoing hallways and calling out her name, she would open up the window seat where she loved to sit and read or stare up at the painted ceiling. Inside there was just enough room for her to hide until the coast was clear once again.

This evening, as on the many occasions before when Ebony sneaked into the study, she found the night drawing in before she even realised what the time was, for she had been reading all day. So far, her grandfather had not discovered her secret place.

Later, when Ebony appeared at the large dining table, she would say, "I was playing in the woods all day, Grandfather."

The girl hated lying to him for she loved him very much, but this was her secret.

Chapter 1

The Defenders of Ia

I didn't know much about my mother as I was only a baby when she went to join the stars. But if I tried – really, really tried – I was sure I could remember her kind, loving eyes, which were brown with splashes of gold, just like my own.

When I asked Grandfather about Mother, he would become very sad; he missed his daughter so much that it broke his heart.

Grandfather would say, "Ebony, your mother was one of the most beautiful women in the whole of Ia – the brightest star in the whole of the kingdom of starry Heaven above. She is looking down on you right now and, if she could tell you, she would say she was very proud. Her love for you will go on forever."

When I asked my grandfather about my father, his grey eyes would become as hard as stone. He would shake his head and reply, "Your father loves you too, Ebony, but his call is to the sea while your mother's is to the stars above."

When I frowned at his words, Grandfather would smile at me kindly, give me a comforting cuddle in his thin arms and tap me on the nose with a long finger. He always knew it would make me smile. "You will meet your father one day," he would say, "and you will finally understand how special you truly are, child."

Grandfather was old, I mean ancient, but he still played games with me. He would jump around like a great big grasshopper, hold me in his long, thin arms and spin me around at a hundred miles per hour. My grandfather loved me and I loved him, but he also worked very hard. Leaving me at our home of Ladon Manor, he would trek the land to trade. I hated it when he left me with the strict Bea. I didn't like her. She was no fun.

Bea didn't live at the manor. In the past she did, but now she lived nearby with her own family. Only when Grandfather had to go away did Bea turn up on our doorstep, laden down with her bags. I know he hated leaving me as much as I hated to see him go.

Bea's brother, Sunny, was nice and he lived at Ladon Manor with his wife, Marsha. Having been friends with my mother, he would tell me stories of how they met and the different lives they once led. Unlike Sunny, who grew up at the manor, my mother used to live in a small town by the sea, called Wood Town. I wanted to know why she had grown up away from Grandfather, but Sunny would never say. He simply replied, "She grew up with her mother."

Whenever I asked Sunny why, he would shake the sandy coloured hair on top of his head and say, "You will have to ask your grandfather."

But I saw how down Grandfather got whenever I questioned him about Mother, so I didn't ask. I didn't want to make him sad again if I could help it. Instead, I would make up stories of my own, of how my mother was a great princess and warrior, leading her army into battle.

I would think up adventures where she had to leave Grandfather to find great treasures. In these tales, my mother saved many of Ia's villagers from fire-breathing dragons and fought strange creatures like the Carrions and the Eternals, as depicted in my wonderful, mysterious old book, which always found itself on the lonely, topmost shelf. I wrote these stories down in my own book and titled it *Ebony's Legacy*.

Grandfather knew of my tales, but he never read them. He would always tell me, "Words have power, Ebony. Always treat them with respect and they will, in return, respect you."

Many nights I sat on Grandfather's lap in front of the roaring fire with our Great Dane, Dominic, by his feet, telling them both about Mother's adventures. My stories always made my grandfather happy. Every time I finished with the words "and they lived happily ever after", he would ruffle my hair and tell me, "You know your mother very well, little one."

And so I continued to read him my tales. My own words, like those in my favourite book, never seemed to jump around. These stories were also my friends.

Mother was known for her art when she was alive and Ladon Manor was full of her legacy. She must have loved my favourite tattered, old book and the painted ceiling just as much as I did.

There were paintings of Ladon, the mighty Star Dragon, with a sun in his mouth, and the bear constellations of Ursa Major and Ursa Minor, spinning in a bluish-black, star-strewn sky. There were also pictures of a cliff rising up from the dark blue sea, a large steam ship and the Crystal City, which now lay in ruins in the bay. But in this painting, the city glittered in the sunlight, as it once did before I was born.

There were also portraits. Some were of my grandfather when he was less grey and wrinkly, and others of my grandmother. Then there were a few faces I did not recognise. I was drawn to two in particular. One was titled 'Chris' and the other 'Blake'.

Once, I asked Grandfather who they were, and he replied, "Stella loved only two men in her life here on Ia. One went to the edge of the ocean for her, while the other understood her soul like no other soul could. Whether either of them loved her more than the other, I could not tell for sure, but I know she loved you most of all." I smiled, for his words made me both very happy and very sad.

The grounds of Ladon Manor were my playground. While the woods provided many trees and bushes with which to build my dens, the kitchen gardens provided tasty snacks when I was hungry. The terraced garden and lawn offered sunshine when the woods were too cool to play in, and the lake was a perfect spot for catching tadpoles and other water-dwelling creatures.

I loved the tadpoles the most, especially when they had both their frog legs and tails sticking out of their backs, as if they were changing before my eyes. I enjoyed creating stories of shape-shifting creatures that could fly over Ia, swim through its seas and run at great speeds across the land. These beings also gave me ideas for my adventures involving my mother.

I always drew pictures to go with my stories. I sketched Mother as a dragonfly, zipping across the lily-filled lakes and ponds of Ia, who then morphed into a gigantic, fire-breathing dragon, smouldering anyone who opposed her.

Grandfather was fond of this story the most. His chuckles made me shake on his lap as he brushed my dark hair back from my face. "Not quite, love, not quite," he would say.

"She wouldn't become a dragon?" I'd ask, making him laugh deep inside his belly.

"No, love. Why, she would become the greatest creature of them all – a mighty Star Bear, whose fur

11

was every colour of the night sky. Stars would shimmer across her body, and she would run so fast that she became nothing but a blue blur. Her loud roar would make her enemies quake in their boots and flee for their lives."

I would smile back and ask Grandfather to tell me more, but he'd shake his head and reply, "You tell me the stories, love. You are the storyteller after all."

So I did. From then on my mother became Ursa Major, the Great Mother Star Bear – princess, adventurer and warrior of the starry heavens. And I, her daughter, Ursa Minor, fought alongside her in every battle. Together, we became the 'Defenders of Ia'.

Chapter 2

Stella Maris

*M*y bedroom was full of Mother's biggest and best paintings. Grandfather had allowed my collection to grow ever since I was old enough to stand, point and say, "Mine." He didn't mind as he liked me to have a huge part of my mother in my life.

The landscapes didn't interest me as much as the other pictures, but I still had a couple. One was of Wood Town and its cliffs. I felt this one was special to Mother somehow. When I looked at the painting, I thought I could feel the wind blowing, smell the gorse bushes, and hear the crows and cows in the fields. My mother was so talented.

Another picture was dark, mainly made up of blacks, reds and greys. From the middle of the darkness a rusty, red creature with hollow eyes and sharp, clawed hands leered out. It was an Eternal. My grandfather hated this picture. He never understood why I chose to have the nightmarish image in my bedroom where I slept at night, but I felt Mother painted it out of pity and curiosity, not fear. Grandfather said it was one of her last paintings before she crossed over to the stars. The rest of the pictures were of Ladon, the Mighty Dragon, Ursa Major and her other companion, Ursa Minor.

Ever since Grandfather gave me my mother's old ring, with 'Stella Maris' carved across its surface, I felt connected to Ursa Minor somehow. Maybe that was why I wrote stories with Mother as Ursa Major and myself as her companion.

13

I asked Grandfather, because ever since I could remember he had studied the stars, gazing up longingly in search of one in particular. When I asked him which one, he told me a story of his own: "For a long time, a star, hung in the night sky. The star pointed the way north and hence she was named Stella Maris, the Northern Star. Sailors were known to use her to navigate Ia's shores. With the Northern Star's help, they knew where they were going even in the darkest of nights. The sailors never hit the hidden rocks or lost their precious cargo. Then, in just one night everything changed – the Northern Star had vanished."

Grandfather paused, his eyes becoming glazed. I knew he was thinking about my mother. He always looked this way when he was remembering her.

***

After a day of hiding in the study, my head swimming with all sorts of creatures, I was eager to know more about one in particular. "Grandfather?" I said, tapping his knee to get his attention.

Grandfather looked down at me for a little while before smiling kindly. He was sitting in his high-backed, green chair with Dominic by his feet. Picking me up off the ground, my grandfather placed me on his lap. Cradling me in his arms, he asked, "So, what story have you got for me tonight little one?"

Snuggling in, I shook my head, as it was his turn to be the storyteller.

"Nothing?" he asked in surprise. I giggled as Grandfather's bushy eyebrows rose higher.

"Tell me about the Eternals?" I pleaded.

He shifted uncomfortably beneath me, and after taking a deep breath he replied, "As long as you promise me that you are not going to have nightmares afterwards?"

I crossed my heart.

"Okay, well, I might, even if you don't," he admitted.

I laughed. "Oh, Grandfather, you are silly."

He chuckled. "Well, okay," he continued. "I suppose you're old enough to hear the story. How old are you now – four?"

"No, silly," I said, poking him in his most ticklish spot.

"Hey, that's unfair! Okay, okay, five then!"

"Five and three quarters!" I cried, laughing at his silliness.

"Whoa! Really?" my grandfather teased.

I nodded smugly.

"Well, okay, I suppose." Stroking his beard, he began, "Before you were born a war broke out, with the Humans on one side, and the Eternals and Carrions on the other."

"They are real then?" I piped up, excitedly.

He nodded. "Oh, sadly so."

"But..."

Grandfather placed a finger on my lips. "Shush, Ebony," he said, smiling. "Let me finish telling you the story, alright?"

I giggled and Grandfather smiled in return as I snuggled against his warm body, ready to hear the rest of his tale.

He continued, "Well, as I told you before, once upon a time the Northern Star hung in the sky, helping those who sailed the seas to navigate Ia's shores. The Northern Star was one of the tools of the trade for many fishermen and sailors, and also for any pirate out at sea."

I squirmed in my grandfather's lap. I loved reading about pirates and their ships, and dreamt of seeing them one day. When I was older, I hoped to join a pirate steamship and sail the ocean.

"Fidget," my grandfather said, chuckling. He tapped the end of my nose, making me giggle. "The pirates and Ia's council didn't see eye to eye. Natural enemies, they hated one another, but to battle the Eternals and Carrions they had to work together."

"Who won?" I asked.

"None of them," he replied.

My mouth hung open in a big 'O', and my grandfather's mouth twitched to one side.

"Huh? But... what?"

Grandfather gave a huge bellow of a laugh, but after a little while he tapped my nose once again. "Yes, it was a bit like that," he said, "but this is the best bit – this is where your mother comes in."

"My mother?"

"Yep," he replied proudly. "You see, your mother was fighting a battle all of her very own. She was helping a lost soul return home."

I gawped and grandfather gave another chuckle before carrying on. "You see, Ursa Minor had fallen a long, long time ago, even before I was born, and he needed help to get home to the night sky."

"She was helping THE Ursa Minor?" I breathed.

Grandfather nodded. "By helping Ursa Minor return home, your mother returned the balance between the worlds. The souls of the Carrions, a flock of foul bird-like creatures, crossed over Ladon's back, ready to be judged. The souls were then destroyed, returned to Ia to be born again, or given safe passage through heaven's gates to join Ursa Minor in his kingdom. Your mother, unlike the many souls entering the afterlife, was given a choice because she had sacrificed everything in her life that was precious to her, including you, her daughter."

I continued to stare at my grandfather, with my mouth still open in a large 'O'.

"I promised your mother that I would look after you. She loved you, her daughter, so much that she didn't want to leave you," he continued, brushing my hair behind my ears with his wrinkly fingers. "Your mother was given the choice of being reborn and forgetting everything she had known, having her soul destroyed or roaming the starry heavens forever, just watching and never being part of Ia again. But no one, not even the gods, should ever underestimate a mother's love, for Stella chose differently. She chose to stay. Your mother is forever more Stella Maris, the Northern Star; guardian of those who dwelled below on Ia and navigator of the night sky."

"Mother's alive?" I asked breathlessly. "Where is she? Why isn't she here with me?" I scrunched up my face as I looked around the dark, fire-lit room.

Grandfather kissed my rosy red cheek. "Shush," he replied. "She chose to be with you, but she can only roam when the stars appear, for she is a spirit of the night and she's all around us. She couldn't live away from you or her beloved Ia. And when you are older, perhaps you'll understand what it all means... Sometimes even I see her."

"You do?"

Grandfather nodded, smiling his familiar smile at me. "Look out for the Northern Star, little one, for when you see it, you'll see her and she'll see you, because you too are made up of the stars."

Chapter 3

Bears Can Run!

That night the wind howled and the rain hammered against my windowpane. Thunder was brewing, threatening. The window frames rattled, waking me suddenly. The fire in my bedroom blew out and the wind whistled down the chimney. A clap of thunder was followed by a flash of lightening, which, in turn, made me scream as I ducked, shaking, under my bed covers.

"Ebony?" my grandfather's voice called out from across the room.

I peeked out from my hiding place and saw a light coming towards me – a candle. "Grandfather," I cried, holding out my arms.

He hurried over. Setting the candle down on my bedside table, my grandfather turned around and slid across my bed beside me. I wrapped my arms around his neck, never wanting to let him go, and he did the same, holding me tight.

"Hey now, don't be afraid of the dark," he said, soothing away my tears. "Remember what I told you – you and your mother rule the night sky."

As I snuggled up against his warm, woolly pyjama-clad body, Grandfather smoothed my sticky-up hair.

"Look," he said, pointing at something outside the window.

Looking, I realised that he was gesturing at the clouds, which were now parting. A star appeared. Despite the storm raging outside, there was hope in the form of that tiny, twinkling light.

"Your mother is watching us," he whispered, kissing the top of my head. "Go back to sleep. Nothing will harm you tonight."

I was soon fell asleep with my grandfather's arms wrapped around me.

***

I sat up suddenly. All was quiet, apart from Grandfather's snoring. The room was very light and cast in a bluish hue, yet there was still no fire and the candle had burnt itself out. Only then did I realise that the light was coming from outside. The storm had stopped.

A voice called to me, "Ebony?"

It sounded familiar, yet unfamiliar.

"Ebony?" the voice called again as the light shimmered slightly.

Slowly, I lifted my grandfather's protective arm and eased myself out of bed. Finding my woolen slippers nearby, I quickly placed my feet inside them and wandered over to the double doors that led on to my balcony.

"Ebony?" the voice called once more, and without hesitation I flung open the doors.

I gasped aloud for the night sky was alive, awash with colours I'd never seen before. Swirls of brilliant particles collided into one another as shooting stars whizzed off across the sky in balls of blazing fire. The constellations themselves stared down on me.

I couldn't see Ursa Minor, but I wasn't surprised as Grandfather had told me once that only those who crossed over to heaven could see him. However, Ursa Major, the great Mother Bear, gazed down on me with her big, brown, gold-flecked eyes. My shocked expression seemed to be reflected in her giant iris. Ursa Major made me feel very small and yet very loved – I was home. Next to her, the mighty serpent, Ladon, holding his fiery orb, fanned himself across the starry space. He, however, did not look at me.

"Ebony?"

I looked to the north in the glorious night sky and there she was, the Northern Star. At first it was dim against the abundance of colours, but then it grew brighter and brighter, bigger and bigger, and closer and closer. As the star drew near, I saw a lady dressed in a star-clustered, blue dress. She landed ever so gently, one foot and then the other. Around her, the ground was not wet, even though it had been raining mere hours before, but instead a light coating of snow drifted down around her.

I raised my eyes slowly and as they met those of the lady in front of me, I saw my own reflected back. This beautiful woman was my mother!

She was everything that Grandfather had described. Her hair was much lighter in colour than mine, a reddish-brown, yet we looked the same. We had the same nose and smile, and even identical eyes. She was slightly taller than I expected, but that didn't matter. She was my mother after all.

"Ebony," she sighed, flinging her arms open and dropping to one knee.

As I ran forwards, she caught me and stroked my hair.

"Mother," I cried. "Why didn't you come sooner? I missed you."

"I missed you too, sweetheart," she replied, kissing the top of my head.

Even though it was snowing all around us, I didn't feel cold. I looked up and the night had returned to the way it had been before. A clear sky full of twinkling stars.

"Come with me?" my mother asked, standing up and holding out her hand.

I hesitated, glancing back through my balcony doors. "What about Grandfather?" I asked. I could see him fast asleep on my bed. "Can he come too?"

My mother smiled a smile I would never, ever forget. "No, my child, I'm afraid, not this time. He must stay here and mind the manor."

"But..." I looked back at him again, feeling torn. "What if he wonders where I've gone? Won't he miss me?"

Smiling, my mother knelt down in front of me once again. "You dear, sweet child, of course he will miss you, but you won't be gone long. Look!"

I looked up to where Mother pointed northwards. Once again, Stella Maris hung in the night sky, shining even brighter than before. "I promise he will know that you are safe, for he'll know you are with me." I watched in delight as she crossed her heart.

I nodded and she rose. Taking my hand, Mother walked me to the end of my balcony. As we reached the stone pillars, I paused, looking over the rough, stone railing. "There's no way down," I told her.

Perhaps she had forgotten? After all, it had been a long time since my mother visited her home, but she did not seem to be listening. I watched in awe as she stepped up on to the railing and before I could stop her, she stepped off!

My mouth fell open in a very large 'O', for instead of falling, my mother hovered in mid-air. Intrigued, I leant forward and saw her feet standing on nothing but her snow drift, which swirled at great speed beneath. "Do you trust me?" she asked.

Tearing my eyes away from her magical platform, I looked up. My mouth snapped shut as our matching brown eyes met, and I nodded. Mother reached out for my hand and I took hers without hesitation. She held mine firmly, but with so much care as to not squish my fingers. With a slight crunch, I stepped out on to the platform of airborne snow. I breathed a sigh of relief for I did not fall through.

I jumped, flinging my arms around Mother's waist as we found ourselves sinking lower and lower to the green lawn below. She held me close, but before I could call out the snow parted and our feet landed ever so softly on the freshly mowed grass, leaving my snoozing grandfather in my room way above.

"There," Mother said, brushing my hair away from my face and smiling down at me kindly as she touched my cheek. "Now that wasn't so scary, was it?"

Grinning back, I shook my head. It was silly of me to feel scared. "Can we do it again?" I asked excitedly, which made my mother laugh out loud.

***

The snow continued to fall around us as we walked hand-in-hand in silence down the driveway from the manor. I looked at my mother and she looked back at me. We couldn't stop smiling together. I had my mother back! Soon we reached the end of the drive and found ourselves on North Road.

"Now don't be frightened," she said, stepping away from me. I nodded once and she let go of my hand. I so wanted to take hold of it again, but I kept my word.

Mother stepped back until she was far enough away that the snowdrift no longer fell around me. As soon as I was outside their circle, the snowflakes littering the ground rose up, swirling in little whirlwinds, surrounding her and shielding her from view.

I tried to reach forward as I didn't want her to leave my sight again. After all this time apart, I didn't want her to disappear, but her voice came to me, echoing slightly, as if she was talking inside my head. DON'T BE FRIGHTENED, MY LITTLE ONE.

I pulled my hand back. As I did so, the snow parted and there stood my mother in her Star Bear form! I saw that the bear's fur was just the same as in the story my grandfather had told me. She had fur ranging from the blackest of blacks to the bluest of blues, and different shades of purple. Stars strung themselves across her body, of which the brightest was the plough-shaped constellation, just like Ursa Major's and Ursa Minor's. Her body, tail and nose were wolf-like, but her ears gave her away as being a bear.

I ran forwards and hugged her, the bear gently cradling me against her body with her chin as she hummed me a lullaby. MY EBONY, she seemed to say in my mind. After a short while my mother turned her body so that she stood beside me. Looking into her big, brown, loving eyes, I instantly knew what she wanted me to do.

"You want me to climb on to your back?" I asked, my voice quivering slightly, as I pointed to her back, way up high.

She nodded and knelt down. I swung one leg over and then finding no reins, I held on tightly to her shaggy fur. Would this be like riding a horse, I wondered. Mother in her Star Bear form looked at me, her lips twitching to one side as she stared with her soft brown eyes in which stars swirled and circled, full of wondrous joy. HOLD ON TIGHT.

As I clung to the Star Bear's night-coloured fur, stardust trickled over my nightdress. She leapt forward and started to run, faster and faster, until we were just a blue blur. At first I was afraid as we were travelling at such a great speed – the sea air whipped our faces, trees and houses zoomed past, and scenery blended together as one – but soon I was loving every moment of it!

Through the woods, the Star Bear leapt from tree root to tree root with ease. Not seeing any predators, I remembered Grandfather telling me how Mother's enemies would quake in their boots with fear at her mighty roar. I tugged on her fur to get her attention.

25

She tilted her shaggy head back slightly as I whispered in her ear, and she let out a funny kind of laugh. Giving a toothy grin, the Star Bear flashed her sharp, white teeth at me, but I wasn't afraid, for she was my mother and I her daughter, after all.

Approaching the high cliffs, we skimmed the topmost edges. The Star Bear took a lungful of air and with one mighty bellow she made the cliff tops shake. The sea birds cried out in alarm and flew away as quickly as their little wings could carry them. The sea quietened and the waves stood still. My ears rang for a long time afterwards, but I whooped with excitement for my mother was truly the Defender of Ia, just as in my stories.

Before long we slowed to a trot and found ourselves on a pebbled beach. The sun was about to rise and I could feel mother's Star Bear's form shimmering beneath me. She knelt so that I could jump down on to the shingle. I stepped away and once more she transformed into human form. Swirls of snowdrifts littered the pebbly beach around us both as we said our goodbyes.

"I will come again when it is time," Mother told me, her voice slightly fainter now. The first of the sun's rays were about to break Ia's surface. "You need to go quickly – all will become clear very soon," she added urgently, pointing behind me.

Out of the gloom, a small hut appeared with a candle set in one of its windows.

"I don't want you to go," I cried, clinging to my mother tightly.

"I don't want to go either, sweetheart, but night is fading and the time for the sun to rise is fast approaching. Remember, I will always be watching over you. Go, my little Ebony, make me proud."

The sun hit my face and just like that my mother was gone.

Chapter 4

The Beach Hut

I turned back to face the odd little hut, which sat at the top of the shingled beach. A small, white picket fence had been hammered into the ground around the front garden, which was not planted with flowers, but full of pebbles instead. They wound their way around in a spiral, making the area look nice and colourful.

I followed the pathway, which was made of blue stones, and noticed that some were red, surrounding smaller, yellow ones. As I gazed, I also saw some larger green stones clustered together, outlining the picket fence, which reminded me of little hedgerows. More of the smaller, yellow ones were surrounded by purple, pink and orange stones. It was as if I were standing in a miniature garden made of multicoloured pebbles. It was perfect. Whoever made it was very clever indeed.

As I reached the steps to the hut, my hands clenched into tight little balls and I started to shake.

BE BRAVE, MY LITTLE EBONY...

Mother's voice was all but a whisper on the sea breeze. But when I looked up in the early morning light, I could see the Stella Maris, the Northern Star, my mother, shining high above. I smiled up at her and she twinkled back, winking. She was watching me and I no longer felt so afraid.

Climbing the wooden steps to the door of the hut, I knocked three times. A few seconds passed before the door slowly creaked open.

"Who's there?" asked a gruff male voice.

I squinted to try and see the man's face, but it was far too dark inside. "Please sir," I replied. Unsure of what to say, I told him my name instead.

"Ebony Night, you say?" he asked.

The door creaked loudly as the man swung it open a little more. The owner of the hut filled the doorframe. He seemed too big for it, as if he had outgrown it long ago. The man scratched his bushy, matted beard as he stared down at me, and I up at him.

The huge man had one eye as the other was covered with a shiny, metal patch. When I looked down at his feet, I noticed that he only had one leg as well.

Well, he did have two, but the other one wasn't real – it steamed and billowed with wisps of smoke and puffs of warm air.

The same yellowish metal that covered his bad eye also plated his magical boot. Behind the bottom of his heel, I spotted a little roaring fire. The door of the furnace was closed, but there was a little porthole, so you could see inside.

This giant of a man who was too big for this little beach hut with its picket-fenced, pebble garden was a pirate! I was shaking again, but I wasn't frightened; I was excited! "So, little Ebony, your mother sent you?" he asked me.

I nodded.

The pirate reached to the side of the doorframe and I heard his keys jingle as he attached them to his belt. Fixed to the leather I saw a number of fascinating little tools of all shapes, sizes and colours. I wanted to ask the man what each one was for, but he suddenly stepped towards me, making me step back in surprise – I slipped, falling on to my bottom.

I watched the pirate from where I sat on the blue-pebbled path, surrounded by the white picket fence, close to the door of the tiny hut, which seemed too small for him.

"Right," he said, reaching out his hand for me to take. "Let's go find your father." And with one great big heave, he lifted me easily back on to my feet.

I walked alongside the huge pirate with the magical boot to the other end of the pebbled beach. As we reached the point where the sea met the cliff, he placed two fingers in his mouth and whistled three times. The whistle was so loud that I had to cover my ears. The sound bounced off the cliff face like a bouncy ball.

"Who are we waiting for?" I asked.

The pirate raised his hand and all went quiet. Then there was a flash of red to our right. I turned, but whatever it was, it was much too quick for me to see. A flash of red to my left soon followed, and then a bird dropped down on to a small boulder in front of us with a gentle plop.

The bird was quite big in size and red all over. It had a long tail, which fanned out every now and then, and it looked very pleased with itself.

The pirate chuckled and searched the many pockets of his waistcoat for something. Upon finding what he was looking for, he offered the red bird his arm to perch on. The creature fluttered up and landed there with a soft plop.

I thought it must be very hard to land so smoothly with a tail that long. Watching the bird fan out its tail, I spotted another two feathers underneath, which were long and fluffy. On the end of each one was a red and white eye.

"This is Scarlett. She is a Fire Crow."

My mouth fell open in a large 'O' as I stared at the beautiful bird. "Wow!" I breathed in amazement, making the pirate smile.

He turned back to the Fire Crow with two tails, one fluffy and one like a fan, and said, "I need a message sent, Scarlett."

The pirate took a small roll of paper from a pocket in his coat and gave it to the bird. She held the piece of paper in her little beak and took off. In a flash, Scarlett was flying across the ocean so fast that she became a fiery, red streak.

"And now," said the pirate, "we wait."

We waited and waited for an age, but nothing happened.

The huge bearded pirate with the magical boot, who lived in the hut that was much too small for him, wouldn't tell me anything! He kept laughing and saying, "Just wait and see."

I sat on the small boulder that Scarlet had landed on and crossed my arms. I was very cross with the pirate as I didn't like it when adults refused to tell me anything. As the sun rose higher in the sky, the Northern Star shone more brightly than ever. My mother couldn't walk in the daytime, but it made me happy to think she was watching over me.

Then I saw something where the sea met the sky. Standing up, I clambered on top of the boulder for a better look. "What's that?" I asked the pirate, pointing at a plume of smoke rising from the sea.

He also rose from where he had been sitting, but he didn't need a boulder to stand up high. "That, little

Ebony," he replied, "is the finest vehicle that sails the high sea. She is called the *Fire Crow*."

The *Fire Crow* docked a little way out to sea from our pebbled beach. A huge ship made of wood and shiny metal with plumes of smoke billowing from its metal, tubular chimneys. Gigantic, round paddles swung the vessel around until it sat in line with the pebbly beach, where the pirate and I stood watching.

I heard a shout and saw a gleam of yellowish gold as a group of men threw an anchor overboard. Men ran back and forth on the ship for a little while longer before lowering a smaller, wooden boat into the water. Two men came towards us in this rowing boat. One was rowing while the other stood at the back, looking straight at me!

The boat clattered up the pebbled beach before coming to a dead halt and the two men jumped into the salty surf. As they splashed their way towards me, I saw that they were pirates, just like the one I had found in the tiny beach hut with its pebbled garden and white picket fence.

One wore a shirt, roughly-cut dark trousers and brown boots, which were way too big for him. The other, who was dressed more smartly, seemed to be in charge as he stood upright and walked with confidence. This second man wore dark brown, fitted trousers tucked into shiny, black boots and a long, high-necked coat, which had large buckles along the arms and shoulders. The bluish-black coat fanned out slightly.

He must be the ship's captain, I thought.

The 'captain' kept watching me. I recognised him now as Blake, the man in my mother's paintings. But, unlike those, this version of the captain of the pirate steamship *Fire Crow* had a deep scar running from his right brow down to his cheek.

"Ebony Night?" he asked. Blake's voice sounded stern, but then he was a captain after all.

I swallowed and nodded.

"Daughter of Stella Night?"

I nodded again.

"Daughter of the land, sea and stars?"

I frowned, not understanding.

The captain smiled. I liked his smile – it went up one side. He seemed a trickster, like Grandfather, and I knew that he and I would be friends forever. As Blake grinned, his sea-blue eyes flashed and they looked kind. He wanted to be my friend also, so I grinned back.

"Come with me," he said, holding out his hand.

I wasn't scared of this pirate captain of the steamship *Fire Crow*, so I skipped forwards and took hold of his fingers. Captain Blake's hand was rough, but very warm, and salt coated his fingers. I imagined him spending many hours on deck, looking out to sea as he ordered his men to their stations. The man carried me in his arms through the surf so that I wouldn't get wet and helped me aboard the tiny rowing boat.

The pirate I had met in the small hut with the pebbled garden, framed by a picket fence, waved his hat at me. "Good luck!" he called from shore as the other pirate in the boat rowed Captain Blake and me towards the steamship *Fire Crow*.

I was very excited!

Chapter 5

Ruler of the Sea

"**R**ight men!" Captain Blake shouted out. The pirates had stopped working and were staring at the three of us coming on board. I stared back at them, wide eyed, for they were a spectacular sight. A few of them, like the bearded pirate back on the pebbled beach, were clinking, clanking, steaming and whistling as they bent their arms or fidgeted on their feet. Some wore boots or hands made of metal, and a few even had whole arms made up of pillowing pistons. The *Fire Crow* was certainly the finest vehicle on the high seas!

"Back to your stations!" the captain cried and all of the men instantly took notice.

Captain Blake looked scary as he stared around at his crew with a stern look under his hooded brows. Then, a crooked smile slowly appeared on his face as he watched them all for a little while. I guessed the captain was very proud of his men and his ship. Then he turned his gaze on me, and I was relieved to find he was still smiling his crooked smile.

"Are you taking me to my father?" I asked him.

"Come with me, Ebony," Captain Blake said quietly, holding his hand out for mine.

Taking the captain's fingers without fear, I followed him to his cabin situated on the top-most deck. It reminded me of my little old book on its top-most shelf. I wondered if he, too, found it lonely up here.

Around the captain's cabin, portholes showed views of the sea and sky. Where the two met, waves bobbed

37

up and down. Through one of these round windows I could still see her, my mother, the Northern Star. I wished she could be here with me, on board a real pirate steamship with a real pirate captain!

I thought of Grandfather back home in Ladon Manor. Would he be worried about me? Mother said he'd know she was looking after me, but I wished he could see me now.

I turned back to look at the pirate and saw that he was also watching my mother, the Stella Maris, Navigator of the Seas, from his captain's chair behind a large desk. He looked very authoritative in that chair, which was made of all sorts of nuts and bolts. Pulleys and levers stuck out at every angle, half metal, half leather.

I looked back at my mother and saw that we were heading in the same direction. The paddles of the steamship were paddling their way towards her. It made me smile to know she was leading the way.

I stood up straight and Captain Blake laughed gently as he turned in his mechanical chair to look at me. "Awaiting orders are you, little Star Pirate?" He smiled his crooked smile at me and I nodded, which made him grin even more. Looking at me, he scratched his stubbly beard, pondering.

"From now on, little Ebony, you," he said, pointing a finger at me, "are a member of my crew."

Staring at Captain Blake in amazement, I asked, "Really?" I had written stories about being a captain and sailing the sea with my mother, going off on adventures of our own around Ia, battling sea creatures, finding treasure in stricken ships and never stepping ashore for many, many years.

Captain Blake nodded. "Yes." He looked at me for a while, inspecting me some more. First he looked me

38

up and down, and then at my hair and my eyes. "You have your mother's eyes," he commented, to which I nodded. "And your father's hair."

"You know my father?" I asked excitedly.

He waved his arm, inviting me to sit down in the chair in front of him, which I did. "Of course I do. I am your father."

I stared at him. "You're my father?" I asked in a whisper, my mouth hanging open in a large 'O'.

Captain Blake, my father, nodded. "And you, my little Star Pirate, I am in need of your help."

Then the captain of the pirate steamship *Fire Crow* began telling me – his daughter, and the daughter of a Star Bear, Stella Maris, the Northern Star and spirit of the night sky – a story that happened a long, long time ago.

"Before your mother ruled the night skies and I ruled the sea, even before the Great War itself, a labyrinth was created. It ran for many miles, from Land's End to the Oil Fields. The Labyrinth lay underneath the bedrock of the ocean itself. No one truly understands its origins or how deep it truly goes.

"The Oil Fields, based on an island off the south coast were ruled by greedy men, intent on enslaving an ancient tribe of men, women and children, for they believed the tribe was sinful and deserved to be punished for crimes against their god. The men took the Ancients to the Oil Fields, where they would spend the rest of their lives working as slaves. The treatment towards the Ancients was cruel and many died under the rule of the greedy men. It is important to remember, Ebony, to rule through good deeds and not through greed."

I nodded.

Captain Blake continued, "The Labyrinth became a catacomb with chambers full of the sick. In time it became full of nothing but bones. The three gods, Ursa Major, Ursa Minor and Ladon, grew angry and Ursa Minor, the youngest of the three constellations, fell from the night sky to try in desperation to help. The impact created a great wave, which rose up and crushed all those in its wake, washing the Oil Fields clean. But though Ursa Minor's action was meant to be a selfless act, it also had consequences he did not foresee.

"As the gigantic wave washed away the evil men, so it also destroyed the Ancients in its path. The cruelty stopped, but the tribe was destroyed. Only a few members remained, scattered across Ia, hidden from the evil men who had enslaved them and the rest of humankind, either by hiding on ships such as this one, or by sheltering in the Iron Hills. Without Ursa Minor, Heaven's gates were closed and the souls were lost – they fell down to Ia.

"There was a flock of Fire Crows who fed on the algae growing on the Oil Fields. When eaten, the algae gave these birds their fiery red colour. The crows flew upwards and scattered when the wave hit the island, but they were also the closest living creatures to the ever-increasing numbers of falling

41

souls. When the souls fell to Ia, they took the form of Fire Crows and became what are now known as the Carrions. Each Carrion took on the pain, hatred and anger of the lost soul it hosted.

"In the meantime, the bodies of the evil men lay broken and twisted at the bottom of the ocean, but they had been saved by withdrawing inside themselves. Their souls were absorbed into their bones, which lay scattered at the bottom of the sea now covering the Oil Fields. As time passed, the Oil Fields drained and the Eternals rose. As bitter and twisted as the lost souls of the Carrions, the two became mutual allies. There they waited, claiming the Oil Fields back as their own, and planning their descent on the mainland of Ia until the Great War came and they fell once again," said Captain Blake.

I looked up at him and his sea-blue eyes grew dark as stormy waters. I could see how his crew would find him frightening – my father, the other Defender of Ia.

The pirate captain took a deep breath and carried on with his story. "Your mother, Stella, returned Ursa Minor to the heavens above and, in turn, balance was restored. The gates were pushed wide open and the lost souls of the Carrions returned to their rightful places, but choice was the key. The Eternals chose to stay while the souls of the Carrions had no choice but to fall. We know the Eternals are still out there, but they are very weak. We, however, are not. When war calls again, your mother and I will be ready. One day, when the time comes, we will unite and strike once again, and this time the Eternals will not be coming back."

I stared at my father, the captain of the *Fire Crow* and Ruler of the Sea, in awe.

"But," he continued, lifting up his finger and looking straight at me, his sea-blue eyes swirling with the ocean's power, "there was also another soul that

43

was left behind – a little girl. She, too, chose to stay and walk the Labyrinth, comforting her friends and family back in the day of the rule of evil men. Now that her task is done, she is lost. She's very lonely and confused, Ebony. She seeks only companionship.

"Lately, she has been travelling further into the mines of Ia. The tunnels of the mines interlink and it is a well-known fact that all of the roads underground eventually lead to the Labyrinth. We would not ask anything of you, Ebony, if we knew we could deal with her ourselves, but she keeps luring miners to the darkest abyss of the maze, trapping them there through fear and confusion, and forcing them to stay with her for all time.

"Ia depends on the miners to fuel our defences and our supplies are running very low. You see, my little Star Pirate, my power is dependent on the sea while your mother's depends on the night sky, but your power rules over all three – the land, sea and stars united. You might not understand or even believe in your powers just yet, but you have to trust that they are there to guide you in this task.

"It breaks the hearts of myself and your mother to ask this of you, but you are our – and the people of Ia's – only hope. We need your help to seek this lost soul. Give her peace, my little Ebony. Reach down deep inside yourself and, most of all, become the bravest you've ever been. Your mother and I will be watching, and waiting for your return."

Chapter 6

The Labyrinth

The *Fire Crow* anchored a little way from shore. The pirates lowered a boat containing my father and me into the breaking waves below. As we made our way over, I noticed two tin mines halfway up the cliff, grey against the dark face whose jagged rocks reached out towards us. The cave's entrance was very narrow and reminded me of the windows in Grandfather's study, reaching from the top of the cliff down to the sea below.

Way above us, Stella Maris hung in the sky. Mother's star shone down on us so brightly, lighting the way, and I knew we were safe. She was guiding us towards the dark entrance, to the little ghost girl waiting within.

I wasn't scared… not one bit.

As we came closer to the cave's entrance, I could see a pathway carved into the cliff face, leading inside. It must have been ancient as the granite path was eroded here and there by the beating sea, leaving deep, dark pools of salty water.

Father found a safe place to dock our little boat and helped me to climb out. "Ebony?" he asked, placing a hand on my shoulder.

I turned to stare up at him. He looked worried as he glanced up at my mother's star, which was now coming down from the starry heavens. When he looked at me, I knew he was trying his best to be brave as well. I hugged him and he hugged me back.

"Ebony, you must promise me that you'll be careful. Listen to your heart and you won't go far wrong."

I stepped back, crossed my heart, and replied, "I will, Father." I stood straight as I spoke, because I wanted to show him how brave I was trying to be.

Captain Blake smiled his crooked smile and gave me one last hug before we walked inside the dark, mysterious cave. He led me a little way inside and it reminded me of the ballroom in Ladon Manor. The ceiling was very high and the walls so far apart that we could have easily fitted the *Fire Crow* inside if it had not been for the narrow entrance.

I held on to my father's hand and he gave it a quick, reassuring squeeze. "It's natural to be afraid of the unknown," he told me, our footsteps echoing as we walked. "But you are my little Star Pirate, so I know you will be the bravest pirate I have even known."

I nodded. Father said the girl was lonely and only wanted companionship. If I was to help her find her way back to her home and family, I couldn't be afraid. I let go of my father's hand. He stopped walking and seeing my expression, he nodded approvingly.

My father's crooked smile was back. "That's my girl," he said.

He turned to walk on, but I skipped forward and soon overtook him. I heard him chuckle. Although I didn't know what he found so funny, I joined in. I liked his laughter.

**

Captain Blake only stopped when we could no longer hear the sea. "This, my little Star Pirate, is where I must leave you." The captain of the *Fire Crow* and Ruler of the Sea looked back in the direction we had come.

"I understand," I replied. Walking up to him, my arms wrapped themselves around his middle. I knew he belonged to the sea and the sea to him. "You should go," I said. "I'll be okay."

Father looked down at me for a little while and I stared back up at him. His scar stretched when he smiled. His eyes were the deepest blue, swirling with the tidal currents of his deepest thoughts. How I loved that!

He removed his arms from around me and placed the one lantern he had brought with us on to the floor. "Now," He said buttoning up the top-most button on my dressing gown, "remember that you must trust in your powers to find this girl, Ebony. She doesn't like

47

the light much and won't appear to you unless it's dark."

My father gazed into my brown, gold-streaked eyes with his own deep blues. I stood up straighter. I was the Star Pirate, daughter of the *Fire Crow's* captain and, after all, who had ever heard of a scared pirate?

He smiled his crooked smile, reminding me of my mother in her bear form when she gave a big, toothy grin. I giggled.

"What's so funny?" my father asked me, but I shook my head. He ruffled my hair and I giggled some more, spinning around to get out of reach.

I imagined that when I finished helping the girl to find her way home, my father would be able to come and live with me and Grandfather, back at Ladon Manor. I was sure he would help to build my dens, play tag with me every day, and jump around like a giant grasshopper, just like my grandfather did in our games.

I pictured my mother reading me bedtime stories. Coming down when the stars came out to play. She would cuddle me as I fell asleep in her arms. Or, I could stay up late and sneak out of my room to meet her under the star-strewn sky. We would go running in the moonlight with me riding on her back, snuggling into her stardust fur, which would keep me warm while the world passed us by in a nightly, blue blur.

I grinned up at the captain of the *Fire Crow*, Ruler of the Sea, my father, and he smiled down at me. "Now go, my little Star Pirate, and help the girl to find her way home."

I waved as I left him standing by the lantern, and he waved slowly back.

Turning the corner, everything suddenly went black. I walked on, further and further into the cave. It narrowed into a tunnel and the sound of my footsteps bounced off the walls. I could hear squeaking and scuttling around me, but I wasn't afraid… not one bit.

One footstep after the other, into the darkness I went, walking straight because I was the daughter of the captain of the *Fire Crow* and Ruler of the Sea. Also the daughter of a Star Bear, the Stella Maris, Ruler of the Skies and Protector of Ia.

I had to be brave, like my father told me. I, Ebony Night, was NOT afraid!

Chapter 7

Misty

I hit something solid and screamed. I spread my hands out in front of me, feeling something hard and slimy beneath my fingertips. Screaming again, I tucked my arms in, turned and ran the other way, only to bump into something just as hard and just as slimy. I collapsed on the ground, all of my bravery left far behind, and I began to sob.

Suddenly, a green, glowing mist appeared and started swirling around me.

"Why are you crying?" asked a girl's voice.

I stared at the mist swirling at my feet. "H-hello," I said, but there was no answer. "Is anyone there?"

"Why are you crying?" the girl asked again.

I held my breath and rubbed my eyes. "I'm not," I told the mysterious voice.

"Yes, you are. Now why are you crying?"

My eyes followed the mist as it started to rise, rotating in front of me. It was alive! I watched it swirl around the bend in the tunnel and that was when I saw a green light heading towards me. It was coming from a lantern just like the one my father had been carrying.

"Father?" I asked with all my fingers and toes crossed.

I saw a hand reach around the edge of the cave wall and another one holding the lantern. The fingers were wrinkled and old looking, long and thin, just like my grandfather's, but unlike his, the nails were pointed. Then I saw her face. This person was definitely neither Father nor Grandfather – it was the lost ghost-girl! I took a deep breath.

50

"Please don't scream," the voice said. It was coming from the strange creature walking towards me. "I won't hurt you."

I swallowed, my scream settling in the bottom of my stomach. "I won't," I breathed.

The girl smiled and moved closer, allowing me to see her more clearly. She was the same height as me, perhaps slightly taller, but she looked nothing like me. My eyes were brown, like my mother's, but hers were as big as dinner plates and as black as the cave itself. Her smile wasn't friendly at all. The girl had some teeth missing from her skull-like face and her hair draped down like tattered curtains. Mist rolled down from her mouth and the lantern, pooling on to the floor and swarming around our feet.

"Are you the lost ghost-girl?" I asked.

"Lost?"

I thought her voice did not go with her face as it sounded too kind. Maybe we could have been friends when she was alive as she sounded nice enough.

The girl shook her head, swishing her lanky, dark hair back and forth. "No, not lost... at least I don't think so."

"Where is your family?" I asked.

"I-I d-don't know," replied the girl, sounding upset. "I-I think they were here."

I frowned. "Don't you remember?"

Shaking her head, she started to cry. I remembered Father's words: "She's very lonely, Ebony, and seeks only companionship."

The girl's cries filled the cave until I had to cover my ears, for they echoed loudly. The mist increased, rising up to my knees.

"Please don't cry," I called, as loud as I could over the noise. "I'll... I'll help you."

"You will?"

Slowly, I took my hands away from my ears and when I realised the noise had stopped, I lowered them and nodded. "Yes, I promise."

The girl smiled at me with a gappy grin, and jumped up and down with excitement, making her green mist-filled lantern bob.

"Oh, thank you!" she cried and then hugged me.

As the girl wrapped her arms around me, I noticed that they were like her face – thin and bony with a greenish tint. I had to stop myself pulling away; after all, I was the daughter of a Star Bear and a pirate captain. Whoever heard of such a person being scared of a ghost? "This way," I said, leading the way.

I didn't have a clue how we were going to find the ghost-girl's family, but perhaps if I found Father, he would be able to help. Or if Mother was around, maybe she could run really fast and help us find them.

The girl took my hand. Hers felt cold and bony, but I knew I shouldn't pull away. To do so would be very mean and only make her cry again. Good manners are a sign of a true lady and gentleman, Grandfather always told me.

I squeezed the girl's hand, reassuring her in the way my father had shown me earlier. "What's your name? Mine's Ebony," I asked the strange, green-glowing, mist-swirling ghost-girl as we continued to walk along the echoing tunnel.

"I-I'm n-not sure."

"Well, let's see. I like the name Connie, how about you?" I asked, turning my head around to look at her skull like face.

The ghost-girl's large, dish-like eyes stared at me unblinking and she shook her black curtain-like hair.

"Okay," I sighed. "Bernice? Annabel? Kelly? Shelly?"

Again, the ghost-girl shook her boney head.

"Dominique? Sarah? Shakia? Jessica? Jessie? Beth?"

Once more she did not agree.

I shook my own head and asked, "What are we going to do with you?" I smiled, because it was something Grandfather usually said to me.

I continued walking at a fast pace with the ghost-girl's bony hand still clasped firmly in mine. Along the way I suggested even more names, but she did not like any of them. I watched for a moment as the strange green mist rolled from the ghost-girl's mouth and the glowing lantern. The strange vapor circled our feet, and with each step it was sent whirling into the stagnant air.

"I've got it," I cried, coming to an abrupt halt. "Misty! How about Misty?"

The ghost-girl's eyes shone and grew even bigger. She smiled her gappy grin and I grinned back. She nodded. "Yes!" she replied. "I like it."

With that, we went skipping down the dark tunnel, hand-in-hand and arms swinging, with Misty's strange little lantern and the glow inside of her lighting the way.

Misty and I were now the best of friends. I was going to find my way back to Father, and Mother would be waiting for me. We would help Misty find her family and everything was going to end just like my stories with 'happily ever after'.

Chapter 8

Stardust

*W*e must have been walking for hours. My slippers were now soggy and floppy from the wet ground, so I took them off and left them behind in the tunnel. I didn't mind walking barefoot. I preferred it to walking in soggy slippers.

"Where are the others?" I asked Misty.

"Others?"

"My father said…" I stopped myself. I didn't want to upset her by saying she had been scaring people. "Father said there were others who went into the caves with you."

Misty shook her glowing green head. "No. I wanted to help them because they had lost their way, but they ran away from me. I followed them, but they ran further into the Labyrinth. I don't like it there. I only wanted a friend."

The ghost-girl bowed her head, her hair hiding her skull-like face. As she did so, even more of the strange green mist rolled out of her. I think she was upset, which made me feel very sad.

"I'm your friend," I said, squeezing her hand to prove that I was no longer afraid of her.

"Really?" she asked, grinning. Her dish-like eyes shone brightly. I think she was happy, but it was hard to tell.

"Yeah, I think we'll make good friends," I replied. "You'll have to come to my home. Grandfather will ask Sunny to serve up his best Sunday roast and the woods are great for making secret dens. You have to meet my mother and father, too. I only met them

55

today. I thought Mother was dead, but she is a Star Bear, who can only appear at night when her star is out. As for my father, I thought he didn't like me and kept away, but he was busy helping to defend Ia and its ocean. He is the captain of a pirate steamship called the *Fire Crow*. You will have to come and meet them!" I pulled on Misty's arm. "Come on! I am sure they are this way."

She stopped moving.

"What is it?" I asked.

Misty shook her head.

"What?"

"They won't like me and, besides, I must find my own family," said the ghost-girl, glancing back down the tunnel from where we had come.

"But Mother and Father will be able to help you find your family," I replied. "You are my friend – any friend of mine is a friend of theirs."

"Really?" Misty asked.

I nodded once. "Really."

"But do you know your way back to them?" she asked.

I opened my mouth and closed it again.

"We have been going around in circles," Misty said. "I recognise this part of the tunnel." She let go of my hand and dragged her long, bony finger along the tunnel wall's multi-coloured surface.

I was annoyed. "If you knew this, why didn't you tell me?"

"Because... because I forgot." Misty hung her head and stared down at the floor, her curtain-like hair swaying in front of her face once more. This time the strange green mist rolled out from her eyes, as well as from her gappy mouth and the glowing lantern. "I'm sorry," she sniffed.

Feeling bad, I reached forwards and took hold of Misty's free hand. "That's okay. I'm sorry I shouted. I was just trying to be brave. And," I added, thinking about what my father told me, "it's natural to be afraid of the unknown." But then Misty was my friend now, so I could tell her the truth. "I'm scared that I won't be able find my way back to my family either," I admitted.

"I'm with you," she replied, squeezing my hand.

I smiled at her. "Thanks. Together we'll find our way, right?"

"Right," she replied, smiling her gappy grin.

"Right," I agreed, "let's walk this way and shout if you think we've gone around in a circle. Okay?"

"Okay," the ghost-girl replied, and we continued to walk forward in the green light encased by her strange and mysterious mist.

***

"Look!" cried Misty after a while, pointing a long, wrinkly finger towards the end of the tunnel. Something glittered brightly up ahead.

"What is that?" I asked.

The ghost-girl shook her head. "I'm not sure," she replied.

We ran until we reached the strange, glittering something covering the floor of the tunnel. I bent down and touched it. It felt dusty. Squinting in Misty's green light, I rubbed my thumb along my finger, and the shimmering dust fell before our eyes. It shone white and swirled into the ghost-girl's own mist.

As we watched, the dust touched Misty, creating a sizzling noise. The green mist dissolved where it

touched the ground and Misty's own feet appeared –
they were bare and whole, just like mine.

"My feet!" she shouted.

"Your feet!" I echoed.

I stooped to gather more of the glittery substance,
creating a light dusting across my hand. It tingled. I
looked at it again in Misty's light. "I recognise this," I
breathed.

"What is it?" she asked.

I glanced at her. She looked very strange, even for
a ghost-girl. Her feet were whole and mist-free while
the rest of her body and face were still in spirit form.

I checked the pocket of my nightdress. "Yes!"

"What is it?" Misty questioned, sounding nervous.

"Do you trust me?" I asked.

The ghost-girl's eyes grew darker and larger, but she nodded. "I trust you, my friend."

I smiled. Taking a handful of the glittery substance from my pocket, I scattered it over her. The sizzling noise was louder this time as the ghost-girl's mist dissolved before my eyes, as did her strange green light.

"What did you do?" she squeaked in the dark, reaching for my fingers.

I took her hand and it felt different: warm and whole! Reaching into my pocket, I removed a little more of the sparkling light, and blew it towards the wall. The particles of dust stuck to the slimy rock, lighting up like glow worms. Misty's eyes met mine and I smiled.

"I made you *you* again!" I laughed, holding up Misty's hand, so that she could see it in the light of the stardust.

Her eyes grew in size, yet they were no longer black, but green and normal. Turning her hands this way and that, Misty stroked her hair, which was now golden, and felt her face and teeth. She was no longer a ghost-girl, but a real girl, just as she was before she chose to stay here for her friends and family all those years ago. I thought Misty was very brave and I was glad I to have chosen such a friend, even if she had frightened me at first.

"What is that stuff?" she asked. Her voice was the only thing that had stayed the same.

"It's stardust. I recognised it because my mother is a Star Bear and her fur is coated with it. Some of it must have fallen into my pocket while she was carrying me to my father last night. And look," I added, pointing at the tunnel floor in front of us, "it must have been falling out of my pocket since I entered the cave. We can follow it all the way back!"

Misty and I grinned at one another, our smiles now matching. The girl no longer had gappy teeth or a smile that was lopsided. Instead, it was as beautiful as the setting sun. I had gained a new friend and no one would ever be afraid of Misty again. She reached for my hand and I took hers.

Nodding at one another, together we ran down the tunnel, following my mother's stardust home. When we reached the end, I spotted Father's lantern, shining the way back to him. Misty slowed to a walking pace and stopped at the entrance.

"Are you coming?" I asked, unsure why she had stopped.

The girl glanced back into the cave and shook her golden head. She nodded in the direction of the lantern. When I looked, I saw my mother and father waiting patiently for me to return to them. Mother stood on one side of the lantern and Father on the other.

I looked past them and saw the waves crashing against the rocks, the foaming tops white in the starlight, which was now scattered across the bluish-black sky. All three of us were united in one place: father, mother and daughter – the protectors of Ia gathered under one stony roof.

I turned back to Misty. "They are my mother and father, who I told you about. They won't harm you. They're really nice."

The girl shook her head again. She tried to step back into the shadows, but I wouldn't let go of her hand. I didn't want to lose her again, my new friend. I looked at my parents, unsure of what to do, and I was relieved to see my mother approach.

She seemed to shimmer slightly, starlight radiating from her body as snowdrifts continued to fall around her. Mother smiled her kindest smile at Misty, who stared back, mesmerised. My mother, Stella Maris, a Star Bear in human form, held out her hand towards my new friend. I saw Misty slowly, ever so slowly, come out of the shadows and reach forwards to take hold of my mother's hand.

She turned and Misty continued to stare up at her, Stella Maris, dressed all in blue with snowdrifts circling her. Mother smiled back, and then looked at me and her smile grew even more. I beamed and raced forwards to hug her, and she hugged me back with her free arm.

"Missed me?" she asked.

I was so happy to see my mother. "Loads!" I replied.

She kissed the top of my head. "I missed you too, my little Star Pirate," she said, holding hands with both of us girls. "Now, let's go to your father's ship. I cannot see the stars very well in here."

I smiled broadly at Misty and she smiled shyly back, her cheeks slightly red. I noticed her shaking as we sat down in the rowing boat. My father didn't say a word, but continued to watch us both as he rowed us towards the *Fire Crow.*

"What's wrong?" I whispered to Misty, but she didn't reply. She just shook her head. Perhaps my new friend didn't feel good in boats. I couldn't see why. It felt good to me.

Chapter 9

The Goodbye

*F*ather helped me up the ladder while Mother helped Misty. The steamship was very quiet as it was very late and only a few of the crew members had stayed up to welcome their captain back on board. After reassurances that everyone had returned safely, the tired crew slouched off to their quarters.

My newfound friend, Misty, and I stood at the side of the *Fire Crow*, looking down at the still sea. The ship hummed with energy. Its engines were still and quiet now, but her chimneys still billowed little puffs of smoke. The *Fire Crow*, like her crew, was fast asleep under the starry night sky.

Even though I had known my mother, father, the *Fire Crow* and her crew for only one day, and Misty for one night, I felt like I was home. My only wish was to have Grandfather here with us, and then we could all go sailing around Ia, exploring the sea with my father by day and the land with my Mother in her Star Bear form by night. Maybe they could all come back with me to Ladon Manor where we would live happily ever after, like the endings of my stories.

Father stood in the dark shadows cast by his ship's tall chimneys, his arms crossed over his chest, watching the three of us with his blue-green sea eyes narrowing, thinking deeply.

Misty still hadn't let go of me, and our hands grew very warm. It was strange to think that only an hour ago, she had been a scary ghost-girl with a strange green-glowing lantern, eyes as large as dishes and mist rolling from her mouth.

Mother approached as I was trying to point out the constellations in the sky to Misty. I was gesturing to Lynx, who sat above Ladon, the Mighty Dragon, and Ursa Major, the Mother Bear, when I heard my mother laughing quietly behind us. "What's so funny?" I asked.

"Oh, nothing, love," she replied, tapping my nose gently, just like Grandfather does when I'm telling him one of my stories.

I giggled and Mother smiled back. She glanced upwards and when I looked too, Ursa Major was in her bear form, watching us from afar. Beside her, Ladon's scaly body crossed the heavens, his sun and horn-rimmed head hidden by folds in the bluish-black skies above. Behind the curtains, I could just make out another Star Bear – Ursa Minor himself!

I felt Misty tremble beside me. Turning around, I found my mother kneeling in front of her once more. "Abigail," she said gently.

I frowned as Misty looked at my mother, a Star Bear in human form, with snow swirling around her, in complete surprise. I was going to ask my mother who she was talking to, but she held up her hand to quieten me while keeping eye contact with Misty. "Abigail? That is your true name, is it not?" she asked. My mother's voice was kind enough, but like my father's, it held authority.

The girl nodded.

"Now, Abigail, I'm going to give you a choice and I want you to think carefully."

My mother's snowdrift became fiercer, rushing around the two of them in little hurricanes. I stared in awe.

"Once you choose, there is no going back. Do you understand?" my mother asked, and Abigail nodded.

"Now, would you like to stay here on Ia? I am sure my daughter and her grandfather would look after you."

Abigail turned her gaze upon me and I smiled in excitement, but she didn't grin back. Instead, the girl just looked at me with blank eyes; her ghost looked back at me.

"Or," my mother continued as Abigail and I stared at her, "would you like to see your own family? Ladon will have to give his judgement, of course, but you are young still. I am sure he will take that on board and forgive any of your past mistakes."

I saw Abigail glance behind her quickly before looking back. My mother smiled at her. "I promise you, he will judge you fairly. I give you the word of a Star Bear. I know this is a very hard decision, but you must choose."

Tears glistened on my new friend's cheek. "Abigail," I said urgently, shaking her hand from side to side to get her attention. "Come with me. Grandfather will look after us both. Sunny will make you that roast dinner I told you about. Mother and Father will..."

Captain Blake, who had been watching us intently, stepped out of the shadows. My voice died in the quiet night as our gaze met. He looked at me sadly and shook his head.

"Mother," I said, unsure as to what was happening. I felt even more lost now than I did back in the cave. "You, you two are going to come home with me, right?"

My mother's hands flew to her face and my father placed his hand on her shaking shoulders.

"B-but, I've f-found you now – I can't lose you again!" I cried.

Mother rose and turned her back, her hands hiding her face as her shoulders shook.

"Ebony?"

It was my father whispering my name. This time he knelt down in front of me. I ran into his arms and he caught me, holding me tightly. His buckled coat smelt strongly of the sea air, and it was wonderful. I clung on tightly to the captain of the *Fire Crow*, Lord of the Rise and Fall of the Tides. I never wanted him to let me go.

Father rocked me softly, his hands shifting slightly. For a split second I thought he was going to let go of me, but he only reached for his face to wipe something away. "We don't want you to go either," he said, "but you must return home to your grandfather."

Pulling away, I saw that my father's face was red in the starlight. "We love you very much, your mother and I," he told me, "but I belong to the sea and your mother must return to the stars above."

I hugged Father once more and he hugged me back.

"When you are older, when you understand your legacy, maybe then you can stay with me here, and you will see your mother when the time is right. For now you must return to Ladon Manor and stay with your grandfather," he said.

I began to cry.

"Please don't cry, my little Star Pirate." My father rocked me back and forth, back and forth. "Remember your mother and I love you very much, and that will never change."

He stood and picked me up in his arms. As he stepped away from Abigail, I looked down and saw that her eyes were the same as mine – tears streamed down her rosy cheeks.

Captain Blake made his way over to my mother and placed his hand against her back. "It is time," he whispered into her ear, before kissing her forehead.

I could see that he truly loved her with all his heart. Instantly, my mother's shoulders stopped shaking where my father had placed his hand and in the spot he had kissed her starlight glow turned blue. This blue radiated out from her. The little whirlwinds surrounding my mother merged together, and the snowdrifts grew and grew until she was no longer visible to the three of us.

I had seen her transform once before, but I was still mesmerised. My salty tears stopped in their tracks. When I glimpsed Father's face, he was smiling gently. Looking at Abigail, I saw that her expression once again reflected my own.

I turned around just in time to see my mother's Star Bear step out from her snowdrift. As my mother, Stella Maris, the Protector of Ia, Navigator of the Sea, passed us, she rubbed her head against my father's shoulder and gently touched my face with her leathery, warm nose. My mother looked into my brown, gold-streaked eyes and I gazed into hers.

I watched the stars spin – multi-coloured particles of stardust rushing around one another. I smiled and in return my mother gave me one of her toothy grins, flashing her fangs at me. I giggled and the Star Bear started to hum.

All of a sudden I felt very tired. Yawning, I snuggled against my father, who smiled down at me and held me closer. My mother looked at him for a few seconds and he nodded. Stella Maris in her Star Bear form then approached Abigail, who shook from head to toe.

The girl gazed down at the waves below. Was she going to jump? My mother once again began to hum and the air shimmered. Abigail stopped shaking and her hands, which gripped the edge of the ship, relaxed.

I WON'T HARM YOU, LITTLE ONE, my mother seemed to say as she stood beside Abigail. HAVE YOU DECIDED?

"Yes," the girl replied in a strange, confident voice.

SO BE IT.

"Cover your ears," my father whispered to me, and I did.

Even with them covered, my mother's roar was louder this time than the night before. My mouth opened in a large 'O' as I watched Abigail rise up into the night sky, with my mother following closely behind. She guided the girl on to Ladon's scaly back.

"Abigail!" I called. They both turned and looked down at me from the heavens above. "I hope you find your family."

The girl smiled, her large grin reflecting my own. "Thank you. I will miss you."

"I will miss you too," I called back. "Friends forever, right?"

Abigail nodded. "Right."

We laughed happily, waving to one another as the girl ran along Ladon's back and through the opened gates. As soon as she entered, Ladon pulled his head back and looked at my mother, Stella Maris, the Guardian of Ia, Navigator of the Sea. They bowed their heads to one another.

I sighed happily. Abigail had finally found her family, as I had mine, for my father was a pirate, captain of the *Fire Crow*, Defender of Ia and Ruler of the Sea, and my mother was Stella Maris, a Star Bear, also Guardian of Ia and Ruler of the Stars.

As for me, I was the daughter of the land, sea and stars. I knew that I would meet them again on another adventure – an adventure like no other.

The Star Bear's hum started up again as she landed back on the deck of the *Fire Crow*. Mother's song was louder this time. Her stardust fur brushed my face and my eyes grew heavy. I snuggled into my father's warm arms as he held me close. His coat smelt of the sea and it was wonderful.

I fell asleep and dreamt of the three gods sitting in their starry night sky, with my father standing on board the *Fire Crow* waving goodbye and my mother running – running in her Star Bear form with me on her back, so fast that we were just a blue blur.

I awoke to find it was still dark and Grandfather lay snoring beside me, just like when I left with Mother. Had it all been a dream?

EBONY, I heard her sigh.

I got up quietly, careful not to disturb Grandfather, and ran over to the end of my balcony. There she was, my mother, in her Star Bear form with the blackest of black, bluest of blue and all shades of purple running through her magical, stardust fur. She dipped her head and leapt up into the air, leaving a glittering trail behind her.

"No," I told myself, "it wasn't a dream." I waved goodbye.

The End

Coming Soon!

Book 2 in Ebony's Legacy:
The Comet Cat

*E*bony has found her parents. Her father is the captain of the pirate steam ship *Fire Crow* and her mother is Stella Maris, the Northern Star, and a Star Bear of the night sky. But once again they had to return to the stars and to the sea without their daughter.

Longing for a friend, Ebony wishes upon a twin-tailed shooting star. What she does not know is that her wish will soon lead her to the kingdom of the constellations, the Milky Way itself.

One night a Comet Cat visited Ebony…

About the Author

A.C. Winfield (Amy) lived in St. Ives (Porthia) on the west coast of Cornwall, England, for the past 21 years. She now, however, lives in north Devon where most of her influences come from.

At secondary school she was diagnosed with slight dyslexia, which made English and exams a struggle, but determined, she managed to get the GCSEs needed for her college course.

After leaving school, Amy studied an NVQ in photography, and continued her passion for this and art by selling her work at local fairs and events, while sharing her enthusiasm for art with children at schools and clubs.

Since 2006, Amy has had the land of Ia (looking a lot like the outline of Cornwall with influences from north Devon's landscape) floating around and forming inside her head. Characters, creatures and places soon followed the story told to her by Stella.

Along with Stella came Ebony and her legacy.

Amy now uses her artistic and photographic skills to create covers and illustrations for other authors, as well as completing her own children's books.

31424363R00047

Made in the USA
Charleston, SC
17 July 2014